GREAT ILLUSTRATED CLASSICS

CHRISTMAS BEDTIME STORIES

created by
Claudia Vurnakes

Illustrations by
Jesse Zerner

BARONET
BOOKS

BARONET BOOKS, New York, New York

GREAT ILLUSTRATED CLASSICS

edited by
Joshua Hanft

Contents

The nurse suggested a walk in the park.

The Christmas Bluebird

Long ago, in a kingdom far away, there lived a sweet little princess. It was Christmas Eve, and everyone in the palace, from the king down to the youngest servant, was busy with holiday tasks. To keep the little princess from getting in the way, her nurse suggested they take a walk in the park.

The little princess ran and jumped in the snow until she was quite red-cheeked. Her tiny gold crown slipped off, and she looked like any other happy child playing on a winter afternoon.

As she darted around the snow-capped hedges, a flash of color suddenly caught her eye. There, under the bushes, panted a little bluebird, shivering in the cold, worn out from flying against the strong winter winds.

"You poor little thing!" exclaimed the princess. "Nurse? Nurse, come help me, please. I've found a tiny frozen bird!"

But the nurse had met up with a friend and they were chatting on the other side of the park.

"Oh, what am I to do? I have nothing for you to eat, poor thing. You are so weak and so cold, "the princess cried.

Just then, a boy's hand reached down and picked up the tiny trembling creature. It was young Robert, son of the village carpenter. He had been walking home through the park when he heard the princess talking to the bird.

"Let me help, little girl," he said. "I have some bread crumbs here in my pocket the bird can eat. We'll feed her and warm her up. Then maybe she will be able to go on with her journey to the southland."

"You poor thing! You are so cold!"

The princess looked up at the boy, "Oh, the court would be so grateful if you could help her! It would distress us greatly if she had to stay here in the snow. She would freeze to death! We cannot allow that to happen in this kingdom!"

Together, the two children gave the creature a few precious minutes of rest.

The princess used her wool scarf to shield the little bird from the cold, and Robert held crumbs up to her beak so she could peck them. In half an hour, the bluebird was hopping from one child's shoulder to the other's. Soon, she tested her wings in a short flight around the hedges, and finally swooped off to head south again.

Robert and the little girl watched the bird disappear. Then the girl noticed the sky was growing dark.

"Goodness, Nurse will be mad if I stay away any longer. I must return to the palace now, but I want to thank you for helping the

Together, they cared for the little bird.

little bird. I assure you, young sir, your kindness will not be forgotten." The pretty child solemnly shook the big boy's hand, and walked away down the path.

Robert laughed as he headed home in the other direction, "What a funny little girl. She talked to me as if she were a queen. I wonder who she is?"

Just then, he bumped into a very worried-looking woman running down the path.

"Boy," she cried, "have you seen a little girl playing here in the park?"

"Why, yes," he answered. "She just left to look for her nurse. Who is she, anyway?"

"Shame on you, boy. Don't you recognize Her Majesty, the Princess?" and the nurse ran off to look for the little girl.

That night, both children snuggled in warm beds. Under her fine woolen blanket, the princess saw visions of Christmas and bluebirds and big boys. Robert slept under a tattered quilt, the face of a merry little girl

Robert dreamed of the funny little princess.

peeking out at him from the corner of his dreams.

Many years passed, and the little princess grew into a lovely young woman. Because she was kind as well as beautiful, she had many royal suitors from foreign lands asking for her hand in marriage. The princess went to her father in despair.

"Father, what am I to do? There are many suitors calling at the palace every day, and yet I see no one who interests me. I care nothing for riches or power. I want to marry a man who is strong in body and keen of mind. But most important of all, I want a man with a good heart. How can I find that man, Father?"

Together, the king and his daughter planned contests for all the young men in the kingdom. The tests would point them to the man with the strongest body, the keenest mind, and the best heart.

"But Father," the princess worried, "what

"I want to find a man with a good heart."

if I don't love that man who wins the contests?"

"Let us wait and see, child. When the time comes, you will know what is right," the wise king replied.

The foreign princes were sent home and a proclamation was posted at every market and every workplace. The king promised his daughter in marriage to the one man with the strongest body, the keenest mind, and the best heart. All the young men of the land took part in the contests, for didn't everyone, rich and poor alike, have an equal chance?

After a lengthy season of wrestling matches, foot races, and chess games, the king announced that two men had shown themselves to be the best in strength and intelligence. One was the son of a nobleman, blessed with education and courtly manners. The other contestant was a simple young carpenter, handsome and upright, but poor.

"If only I could see into their hearts!"

From a seat by her father's side, the princess searched each man's face.

"I'd marry 'em both if I was you, Princess!" shouted a witty old peasant woman from the crowd. "They's both fine lookin'!"

Indeed, they were. "If only I could see into their hearts," thought the princess. "Perhaps then I would know which man to love as my husband."

The king announced the final test: the man who could make the most beautiful gown for the princess—in one night's time—would marry her on Christmas Day.

The princess turned puzzled eyes to the king, "Sewing a gown? How can this test reveal what is in a man's heart? I should have just married your tailor, Father!"

"Trust in Providence, my dear," her father replied. "I feel we may learn much, watching this final challenge."

Christmas Eve arrived, and the king threw open the doors to a workroom filled

The final test—to sew a gown.

with every kind of fine silk and satin. The two suitors sat down at tables supplied with scissors, thread, pins, and needles. The doors were locked, not to be opened again until dawn on Christmas Day. The king and his daughter settled down on chairs in the hall outside the workroom. A servant pulled back a curtain to reveal a tiny peep hole in the wall. The hole would allow them to look into the room, to watch this final test.

At first, there was a flurry of activity as the young men made their choices from among the cloths of silver and gold. On her chair beside the peep hole, the princess watched their scissors slicing into the fabric. Each slash felt like a knife in her heart, and she whispered a prayer, "Please, give me a Christmas miracle. Let the right man win, the man with the best heart, the man I can love forever!"

Hours passed and the bustle in the sewing room settled down to the quiet of pinning

"Let the right man win!"

and basting. The first suitor, the young nobleman, was busy putting together a gown as bright as the rainbow. The sleeves were crimson silk, the bodice was sky blue, the skirt shone with purple and gold threads, and the collar was a brilliant emerald green. Next, the nobleman selected lace and ribbons and jewels of every description. The princess approved of the lavish choices the young man had made. Did the rich fabrics he was cutting mirror a richness of heart? She watched carefully as he picked up a needle to begin sewing.

First, the nobleman clipped long, long threads of gold. He started stitching. The gold thread certainly sparkled against the rainbow gown, but no matter how carefully he stitched, the thread would tangle. Knots leaped onto his needle, spoiling the seams of the beautiful dress. The princess noticed that he pulled out the tangles with an angry jerk.

Knots spoiled the seams.

Over at the carpenter's table, work progressed more slowly. The young man's rough hands snagged the delicate fabric before him. So many lovely colors, so many choices . . . and yet, it was hopeless. What did he know of courtly jewelled gowns? He was a simple carpenter, not someone the princess would want to marry. Yes, he had done well in the king's other contests, and he had let himself hope that his dream might come true. But now . . .

The carpenter closed his eyes and remembered back to a Christmas long, long ago when he had first seen the princess. He knew she didn't remember, but in his mind, the picture was crystal clear. He saw a boy and a little girl kneeling together in the snow to care for a frozen bird. Through the years, he had secretly watched the funny little girl grow up. His father was often called to the palace to repair broken chairs or to build new closets. Robert always tagged

Robert secretly watched the princess.

along, just to get another glimpse of the princess. He saw her sneak food to a hungry old man, and he heard the kind words she had for even the clumsiest servant. Robert didn't know when it happened, but he knew he had loved her for a long time.

Sighing at the hopelessness of the task before him, Robert finally selected a single piece of satin the color of a sunrise. Carefully he cut out a simple dress. "Some say this is a night of miracles. If only that might be true," he murmured.

Watching from the peep hole, the princess frowned at the plainness of the carpenter's gown.

At that moment, a weak fluttering noise drew Robert to the window. The princess saw that a bluebird lay in the snow on the ledge. The little creature trembled with cold and exhaustion. "Poor thing, come and get warm," said Robert, carrying the bird to his table. He spent long moments gently stroking the tiny

"Could this be the very same bluebird?"

body until the bird was warm enough to hop around. Next, he found some crumbs in his coat pocket and spread them out for the bird to eat.

Memories of long ago suddenly stirred in the princess's mind. Could this carpenter be that same boy . . . ? Could this be the blue-bird . . . ?

"You can fly away now, pretty thing. I must get back to work if I am to win the princess I have loved for so long," Robert said. He picked up his needle and a spool of thread. With a sudden swoop, the bird snipped a very short piece of thread from the spool. Holding the thread in her beak, she flew straight to Robert's hand and slipped the thread neatly through the needle.

The carpenter laughed. "Thanks, little friend. That's a good trick, but I have no time to play. I need a long piece of thread for all the stitching I must do this night." And Robert pulled the short thread out of the

"That's a good trick!"

needle. Quickly the bird grabbed the same short piece and threaded it back.

"You want me to use this short thread, don't you? Perhaps I should try." Robert began sewing with the bird's piece of thread. Slowly, the gold stitches crept down the seams of the plain satin gown. No knots, no puckers, no tangles. Each time Robert ran out of thread, the little bird had another short piece ready for him.

As the night passed, each suitor worked on. The princess watched the nobleman fuss over his long tangled threads, while the carpenter stitched smoothly with his short ones, the bluebird perched on his shoulder.

Long before either man was ready, the first rays of morning crept through the window. The nobleman threw down his needle and grabbed for the straight pins. He finished his brilliant gown trimmed in lace and jewels, but half of it was only pinned together. The other half was spoiled by large

"You want me to use this short thread?"

uneven stitches, with knots and loops of thread, and puckers down each seam. Robert calmly tied a neat knot, and the little bird clipped the gold thread from the last seam on the carpenter's gown. The simple dress was done. Every seam was carefully stitched, but there were no jewels to relieve its plainness. "No Christmas miracle for me," Robert thought sadly.

The king unlocked the door to the workroom as trumpets blared. All the lords and ladies of the court filed in to see the outcome of the king's test. Last of all came the princess, wearing only a bathrobe, ready to try on the gowns stitched by her suitors.

A sigh rippled through the crowd as the king held up the young nobleman's gown. At first glance, it was a lovely thing. The gems sparkled, the brilliant colors shone, and lacy ruffles floated down the front. With a heavy heart, the princess slipped behind a screen and pulled the dress over her head.

At first glance, it was a lovely thing.

"O-h-h! I'm stuck!" she gasped. "Someone help me, I can't move!"

The ladies-in-waiting jumped to help the princess out of her prison of pins. They placed the gown before the king. In the clear light of day, every pin, every pucker, every knotted golden thread showed plainly.

The king frowned. "I fear this gown reveals the true nature of your heart, young sir. No matter how beautiful the outside may be, it cannot hide the knots and tangles of a troubled soul."

He turned to Robert and picked up the carpenter's simple dress. No lace, no tucks, no trimmings, no jewels, just plain golden stitches marching neatly down satin the color of sunrise. With trembling fingers, the princess slipped into the gown and stepped out before her father and all the court. The bluebird flew over and perched on her shoulder. Brightness streamed into the room. It lit up the sunrise satin until the lovely young

Just a simple dress.

woman in the simple dress blazed like a slender candle on a dark night.

"What sight could be more beautiful than this?" laughed the king. "Daughter, what say you? Will you take this good man Robert to be your husband?"

The princess was silent for a long moment, overcome by the strange new feelings leaping up in her heart. At last she spoke. "I am satisfied," she said," that I have found the one man in all the land with the strongest body, the keenest mind, and the best heart. A man is never stronger than when he lends a hand to a poor suffering creature. His mind is never keener than when he listens to good advice, regardless of the source. And his heart is never purer than when he follows his dream, no matter how hopeless it seems."

It was a joyous Christmas wedding, with beautiful carols and bird songs gladdening the hearts of all who heard.

It was a wonderful wedding.

Amber had a very special jar.

The Mason Jar

Amber had a very special jar.

Amber herself was a very special person. She had dark brown eyes that danced when she was happy. Her cheeks were tan and smooth, and her curly hair hung in a thick braid down her back. Little brown curls popped out all around her head, like a halo. But the most special thing of all was Amber's smile. It lit up her whole face. Granny said Amber's smile was like turning on the light in a dark room. Strangers passing on the sidewalk would stop for a second look at the happy young face.

But right now, Amber wasn't smiling. She

was sitting on her bed with a quart jar in her lap, and she was frowning.

Let me tell you about this jar. It was a Mason jar, a glass jar that people use for home-canned beans or strawberry jam. The jar had a wide mouth, large enough for a big spoon. Raised numbers on the side showed cups and ounces. This particular jar was one of the older types. It came with its own glass top. When the jar was full, you put the top on and lifted the wire attached to the neck of the jar. The wire held the top tight.

In days gone by, Mason jars were important because people had no other way to preserve food. They would pack their vegetables in jars, seal the lids, then place the jars in a deep pot of boiling water. This killed the bacteria that caused fresh food to spoil. Today, most people don't bother with canning. It's much easier just to buy cans of food from the grocery store. That's why Amber's granny had given her the Mason jar.

People preserved their vegetables.

"There aren't many of these old jars left, Amber," Granny said. "Every time I see one, I think of Mama June's kitchen. She had shelves and shelves of these jars, each one with something good inside that we had grown ourselves. Cherries, tomatoes, beans, pickles, jam, peaches. U-m-m, um! My mouth waters just thinking about them. Take good care of this jar, and it will really be valuable some day."

The jar was already valuable. It contained $38.52.

For almost a year, Amber had been saving up to buy the guitar in Music City's window. From the first day she saw it, she knew it was meant to be hers. Glossy golden wood, nylon strings white against the dark neck of the guitar. A fancy wooden design around the sound hole, and tuning keys that looked like ivory.

Amber had never played a guitar, but she just knew she could. Especially a guitar like

Amber knew she could play this guitar.

this one. Her fingers already knew how it would feel to press the strings against the frets. In bed at night, she strummed an imaginary guitar, letting the nails of her right hand pluck notes from the strings. Her body already knew how to cradle the instrument, how to lean into the sound until the guitar and the guitar-player became one thing. How wonderful it would be to strum and sing, and strum and sing!

All she needed was twelve more dollars. The guitar at Music City cost $49.99. Twelve dollars would give Amber enough to pay for the guitar, with some change left over for tax. Maybe she would get some money for Christmas. Maybe, maybe by the end of January, the guitar at last would be hers!

Amber had worked hard all year, saving money to put in the Mason jar. In addition to the regular chores she did for Granny, she raked leaves and she did some babysitting. All her birthday money went straight in the

All she needed was twelve more dollars.

jar, and last summer, when she went to the carnival, she only let herself spend $2.50. The guitar was much more important than going on every ride. Amber made some money on their paper route, too. In October, Granny had taken over an early morning route for the Ledger-Star. Granny rolled the papers and put the rubber bands on. Amber delivered them so Granny could stay home while Jamie slept.

Jamie was Amber's younger brother. He had a disease that left his legs too weak to walk on, so he used a wheelchair. Jamie looked a lot like his older sister. He had the same warm brown skin and curly hair. He had a nice smile, too, almost as nice as Amber's. But Jamie was famous for his singing. He loved to sing, and he did it all the time. On Sundays, his sweet clear voice soared above the heads of sleepy church-goers. Mrs. Whidbee, who played the piano, thought Jamie was one of the best singers she had ever heard.

Amber helped with granny's route.

"Have you ever thought about getting some music lessons for that child?" she had asked Granny.

Granny had a hard time just paying doctor bills and keeping food on the table. That's why the Mason jar money was so important. Granny couldn't afford extras, like music lessons or a guitar. Anything special that Amber wanted, she had to save for herself. Like the guitar. Now, just twelve dollars away, there was a problem.

It was Jamie. For weeks, the church choir had been working on music for their Christmas performance at the shopping mall. All the choirs from churches around town got together, and the Saturday before Christmas, they put on a huge program in the middle of the mall. This year, Jamie was supposed to sing a solo in front of all those shoppers. The song was "Go Tell It on the Mountain," and Jamie sounded great. But now he wasn't going to do it. He didn't have the clothes Mrs.

Jamie's voice woke sleepy church-goers.

Whidbee said they had to wear for the performance, so he just wasn't going to do it.

Granny didn't know anything about the problem. Jamie hadn't mentioned it at home. The only reason Amber knew was that Mrs. Whidbee had stopped her in the hall at church and reminded her that Jamie needed a white shirt and a pair of black pants. The choir always wore robes when they sang at church, so clothes had never been a problem before.

It was a good thing that Amber and Jamie were such nice-looking kids, Granny always said with a laugh, because they sure didn't get any help from wearing fancy clothes. In fact, most of their clothes came out of the charity closet at church. Granny always ironed and mended and kept their things spotless, but that couldn't hide the fact that they were all second-hand. Jamie didn't have a white shirt or a pair of black pants because no one had donated any to the closet. Maybe Mrs. Whid-

Amber and Janie wore second-hand clothes.

bee just didn't know that's how it was with them.

That afternoon, Amber talked to Jamie. Or at least she tried to.

"You know, you could borrow a white shirt from one of your friends at school."

No answer.

"Well, what if you just wore your regular clothes? Would that be so bad? Since you're singing a solo, you need to stand out from the crowd anyway."

Jamie blew up. "Thanks a lot! I already stand out from the crowd too much because of this dumb wheelchair! I-I just won't sing at the mall." He rolled off into another room.

That night, like most nights, Jamie sang and sang in the bathroom as he washed up. Amber sat on her bed and listened. "Go-o, tell it on the mo-un-tain, O-ver the hills and ev-'ry-wh-ere . . ."

Everything that Jamie couldn't do because of his wheelchair went into his singing. It

"What if you just wore your regular clothes?"

was such rich singing. On a happy song, his voice bubbled, and when the song was sad, you wanted to cry. But no matter what the song was, you wanted to go on listening and listening. It just wasn't right. Jamie already missed so much because he couldn't walk. It just wasn't right that he should miss his solo because of clothes.

The Mason jar full of dollar bills and coins felt heavy in Amber's lap. She shut her eyes and she could see every inch of the gleaming golden guitar.

"G-o tell it on the mo-un-tain, O-ver the hills . . ."

Slowly, carefully, so it wouldn't hurt so much, Amber closed the door on the idea of the guitar.

The Saturday before Christmas came and Amber was up bright and early to deliver newspapers. She rushed home and ran into Jamie's room.

"Come on, lazy bones! You've got to wash

"Come on, lazy bones!"

up for the choir performance. It's Knock-Their-Socks-Off-Solo Day!"

Jamie pulled a pillow over his head to hide tears. "I'm not going, remember? Get out and leave me alone."

Amber couldn't resist a tad of teasing. "Oh, so Mr. High-and-Mighty is too good to sing with that pitiful little choir down at the mall? Take that, you dirty rat!"

She threw a shopping bag at Jamie's head and ran out of the room.

It was a proud, proud day. The whole choir did a wonderful job. When it came time for Jamie's solo, he rolled his wheelchair out in front of the crowd and picked up the microphone as natural as any TV star. He looked so fine up there in his crisp new white shirt and black pants. Then he opened his mouth to sing. The sweet strong voice grew and grew until it filled every corner of the mall.

"G-o, tell it on the mo-un-tain, O-ver the hills and ev-'ry-wh-ere!"

The whole choir did a wonderful job.

Shoppers all over stopped to listen. For Jamie, Amber and Granny, this was Christmas. Nothing could be any better than this moment. Oh, they had a big meal on Christmas day, and they exchanged the small presents they had bought for one another. But this was it, the shining moment to be tucked away in the heart and saved forever.

Later that night, after Granny had tucked an exhausted, happy Jamie in bed, she came in Amber's room. She had a dollar bill in her hand. Amber watched as Granny dropped the money in the Mason jar.

"Well, it's not an empty Mason jar any more," Granny smiled. "Now it's a ready Mason jar!" And she kissed Amber goodnight.

"Now it's a ready Mason jar!"

Just two days until Christmas!

Happy Birthday, Sandwich Jackson!

"Frankie, honey, I might not have time to get a fancy birthday cake made. Would a cake mix do?"

Mrs. Jackson looked up from the piles of Christmas cookies she was decorating to catch her 10-year old son sneak a big swipe of icing. She lightly popped his hand.

Frankie's temper flared,"Mom, how many times do I have to tell you, call me Frank. I'll be 11 in two days and it's still Baby Frankie. And no, a cake mix is NOT okay. I'm sick and tired of getting squeezed out of a decent birthday just because I happened to be born on December twenty-fifth. I never have my own party. Most of the relatives just get one gift and let it count for birthday and Christmas. Now you don't want to bake a cake. I hate having a Christmas birthday! I just hate it!"

Mrs. Jackson put down the icing tube and glared at her son for a long minute. "Young man, that's mighty ugly talk just two days before Christmas. March yourself up to the attic right now and calm down. And while you're up there, I need you to look for the tree angel. The girls have gotten most of the ornaments down, but they couldn't find that angel we always put on top of the tree."

Frankie shuffled out of the kitchen and opened the door to the attic. He stopped on the bottom step to look into the living room where his three sisters were busy decorating the Jackson family Christmas tree. June and Jean were twins two years older than Frankie, and Emily was four. The three girls

"I get squeezed out of a decent birthday!"

hung shiny balls on the tree as holiday music sang softly from the stereo.

"Hey, Frankie, we got tired of waiting for you. You're too late, now!" June called to her brother.

Jean chimed in, "Frankie, Mom says you have to get the angel down from the attic. For once in your life, would you please try to make it snappy?"

"Gr-eat," Frankie muttered. "They've done all the fun parts without me. I get squeezed out of everything around here. I'm stuck with a Christmas birthday and I'm stuck with two hog sisters. Everybody around here thinks I'm just a stupid sandwich. Sandwich Jackson—that's me!" He slammed the door and trudged up the steps.

Frankie played in the old trunks for a while, trying on weird hats and jackets that smelled of moth balls. "Hello there, Sandwich Jackson, sir," he said, saluting himself in a dusty mirror. With his finger, he

Frankie wrote his new nickname in the dust.

reached up and wrote his new nickname in the dust, "Frank SANDWICH Jackson."

He sighed. It really was hard having a Christmas birthday. Everybody else got two special times a year, and he only got one. It just wasn't fair.

Frankie finally decided to start looking for the tree angel. He rummaged through boxes containing old shoes, buttons, and snapshots. He found the tea set June and Jean had when they were little and put it by the steps to take downstairs for little Emily. At last, climbing over ten years' worth of National Geographics, he found the box labeled ANGEL shoved into a tight corner under the roof. The box was crumpled and one corner had been crushed. Frankie pulled off the lid to see if the ornament was all right. The paint on the angel's faded face had chipped and one wing had broken off in the box.

"Poor old thing," Frankie thought. "Some Christmas angel you are. You've been

It was hard having a Christmas birthday.

squeezed up in that box too long." A quick little smile crossed his face.

"Hey, you're a sandwich angel! Just like me, Sandwich Jackson!"

Memories of the cross words he had spoken downstairs to his mother returned. "Well, it's not fair," he said out loud, looking down at the angel. "I just wish I could have a regular birthday, not a Christmas birthday. Just once, I'd like a normal birthday."

Frankie blinked and looked harder at the broken old angel in his hands. Had he seen a slight movement in the box? And what was that, lingering in the chilly attic air? Was it the faintest echo of a tiny laugh? He shook his head to clear out the confusing thoughts. "You've seen too many Christmas movies, Sandwich old boy!" he told himself.

Mrs. Jackson's voice reached up the attic steps. "Frankie? Frankie, are you up there? Come down please, honey. I need to ask you a very important question."

"Hey, you're a sandwich angel, just like me!"

A very important question? Maybe his mom wasn't mad anymore. Frankie ran downstairs, leaving the angel behind in the attic.

"What is it, Mom?"

"I was wondering, sweetie, what kind of cake would you like for your birthday? Mocha Walnut Fudge or Pineapple Supreme with cherry-coconut icing?"

"I thought you were just going to make a mi—" Frankie stopped in mid-sentence and looked around. Something was wrong. Where were the Christmas cookies his mother had been baking? No messy bowls, no icing tubes, no red and green sprinkles were anywhere to be seen. Frankie hadn't been gone long enough for his mom to clean up this fast.

"Say, Mom, where are all those cookies you were baking?"

"Cookies? I haven't made any cookies lately," his mother said. "I was just planning your birthday dinner. So, what kind of cake do you want?"

Where were the Christmas cookies?

"Um, a-a-, you pick, Mom," Frankie said, an uneasy feeling eating at his stomach. He dashed out of the kitchen.

The feeling grew. Where just half an hour ago Frankie had seen an almost-decorated Christmas tree, there was an empty corner. His sisters were spread out on the living room floor. June and Jean were finishing their homework and Emily was cutting pictures out of an old magazine.

Jean looked up at Frankie and smiled, "Hey, hey, hey! It's the birthday boy. Just two days left. We've got some great presents for you!"

"And wait until you see the cake Mom is going to make, Frankie. It's going to be the fanciest one ever!" June said.

"I've got something for my Frankie, too," little Emily added. "But it's a secret."

Three little beads of sweat popped out on Frankie's nose. What was going here? His sisters were never this nice to him. And

His sisters were being nice.

where were the Christmas decorations they had placed all around the house last week?

Frankie started searching, opening doors and looking in closets. No tree, no wrapped packages, no spools of red and green ribbon, no wreath on the front door, no stockings to hang by the fireplace, not even Grandmother's fruitcake in the refrigerator. Even though he searched all afternoon, Frankie could not find one sign that Christmas was only two days away. June and Jean sure had done a good job of tricking him.

"Ha, ha, ha. Very funny, you guys. Now tell me where you've hidden all the Christmas stuff." Frankie demanded at the dinner table.

The conversation stopped for a second as the family gave him puzzled looks.

Then the talk picked right back up as if Frankie had never said a word.

Finally, right at bedtime, Frankie had a brainstorm. "Of course, the calendar and the radio! Why didn't I think of those sooner?

No signs of Christmas anywhere.

June and Jean might be able to hide every other Christmas thing in the house, but they can't change what's printed on the calendar, and they can't stop the radio stations from playing Christmas songs!"

Frankie rushed downstairs to check the calendar that hung by the phone in the dark kitchen. "Now, let's clear this whole joke up," he thought, peering at the December page in the dim light. He blinked and looked harder. What? He rubbed his eyes and looked again. There it was, the square labeled December twenty-fifth. No matter how hard Frankie looked, he couldn't see any trace of little red letters spelling out CHRISTMAS. He even rubbed the square with his finger. Could the twins have erased the letters or pasted a blank square on top? No.

Desperately, Frank whirled around to the radio his mother kept on the kitchen counter. He flicked it on and began twisting the dial madly. "Please, please," he thought.

Chirstmas wasn't marked on the calendar.

"Let me hear just one note of Silver Bells or White Christmas!"

"Frank, is that you? What's the matter, son?" Frankie's dad walked into the kitchen to raid the refrigerator.

Frankie gulped, "Dad, um, I-a, I'm confused. What happens in two days?"

Frankie's father started laughing. "What's the matter? Are you afraid I'm going to forget your birthday? No way, pal!" And he slapped his son on the shoulder on the way out the door with a glass of milk.

Even though he had tossed and turned all night, Frankie woke up early. It was Christmas Eve, and he had an idea. A crazy one, but something he had to try.

He sprinted through the kitchen on his way to the attic door.

"You're frisky this morning," his mother noticed as she scrambled eggs for breakfast. "Ready for Big Eleven tomorrow?"

She didn't mention that today was Christ-

"Ready for the big Eleven tomorrow?"

mas Eve. Frankie was already taking the steps to the attic two at a time in his rush to get up there and find the angel. All night, he had thought over the strange afternoon. How everything Christmas had disappeared when he found that old angel.

"It's crazy," he thought to himself. "But I'll try anything. It's Christmas Eve, for pete's sake! I've got to find that angel, and make a wish, and get Christmas back for tomorrow!"

By lunchtime, the attic was topsy-turvy. Frankie's face was filthy, and he had rammed a splinter under his thumbnail. No angel. No crumpled box. No sign that it had ever been up in the attic.

At this point, Frankie was frantic. What should he do? No one else in the family seemed to notice that suddenly there was no Christmas. All they could talk about was his birthday coming tomorrow.

He hopped on his bike and pedaled wildly down the street. The Walters had a wreath

It was a crazy idea, but it might work!

on their door, and he could see a Christmas tree in the window at the Greenbergs'. The mailman was delivering packages down the street, and old Mrs. Maynard called out, "Merry Christmas, sonny!" as he zoomed by.

So it really was Christmas Eve, and tomorrow really was Christmas. Only at his house had Christmas disappeared into some black hole. Frankie raced home determined to fix things.

He spent the afternoon and evening locked in his room, wishing Christmas back. He tried every magic word he'd ever heard. "Abracadabra!" "Open Sesame!" "Eeny meeny miney moe!" "IwishIwishIwishIwish . . ." Frankie even wrote down promises:

"Just make tomorrow Christmas, and—

I'll never complain about a Christmas birthday again.

I'll never listen to June's & Jean's phone calls.

I'll keep my room really, really clean.

Christmas Eve everywhere else

I'll eat Mom's broccoli casserole. . . ."

He filled up a whole notebook, but nothing changed.

"Today is Christmas Eve," he thought miserably. "We didn't go to candlelight service. We didn't eat our special midnight snack. Dad didn't read 'Twas the Night,' and we didn't hang up our stockings. What have I done? Oh, what have I done?" He cried himself to sleep.

December twenty-fifth dawned bright and clear. Frankie could tell, even with his eyes closed. He was afraid to open them.

"Let there be a tree," he pleaded silently. "Let there be stockings and presents. Oh, let it be Christmas!"

But what it was, was just his birthday. The first thing he saw when he opened eyes was a sign June and Jean had hung in his room in the night.

"Happy Eleventh Birthday, Frank!" it read, in crazy neon letters.

He went to the kitchen for breakfast.

"Just make tomorrow Christmas..."

Remarkably, the family was acting like this was just another normal day. His mom and dad both hugged him and said happy birthday. Emily gave him a sticky oatmeal kiss. No one mentioned Christmas.

"Mom, Dad, I'm sorry!" Frankie cried silently. "Don't you know it's Christmas? Don't you realize what you're missing?" He looked at his sisters. "Emily, how could I have wished your Christmas away? June, Jean, what have I done to you? I'm so, so sorry!"

"Time for birthday presents!" the twins announced with a grin, bringing in arm loads of brightly wrapped packages. They were the best birthday presents ever - a remote control car from his parents, a boom box from the twins, basketball shoes from his grandmother, and a Louisville Slugger bat from the cousins. But Frankie was miserable. Nothing could make up for no Christmas.

"Hey, you forgot to open my present!" Emily

They were the best birthday presents ever!

shoved a wrinkled brown lunch bag in front of her brother. A yellow feather had been stuck to the top of the bag with about ten staples and three pieces of tape. Another one of Emily's famous junk presents, Frankie chuckled.

"I found you something beautiful up in the attic," Emily said.

Frankie ripped the bag apart like a wild man. The tree angel fell out in his lap. Before his family's startled eyes, he held the angel up to his face and shook it tensely.

"I wish for it to be Christmas again! I wish for Christmas! I don't care that my birthday comes on Christmas, do you hear me, Sandwich Angel? Just make it Christmas, please! Just . . ."

Dots of color shifted and formed new patterns before Frankie's eyes. He was standing up in the attic, looking down at a broken angel in a crumpled box. He rushed downstairs, the box in his hands.

"Frankie, you found her! Girls, here's the

It was one of Emily's famous junk presents.

angel for the tree!" Mrs. Jackson called.

Emily came running to the kitchen. "Oh, she's beautiful!" the four-year old exclaimed, reaching for the doll ornament.

"Listen, Emily," Frankie said. "We need to fix her before you can put her on the tree. Go find some glue and I'll put her wing back on."

As Emily scampered off, Mrs. Jackson came up behind her son and ruffled his hair. "You don't really mind your birthday being on Christmas, do you, honey?"

"No, I guess not. It really makes things special to have Christmas and birthday all sandwiched in together."

A tiny "ting," like the sound of a little golden bell came from the angel box.

"Did you hear that?" Mrs. Jackson asked. "What else is in that box, anyway?" and she reached for the angel.

Frankie just grinned. "Merry Christmas and Happy Birthday to us, Sandwich Angel!" he thought, handing over the box.

The ring of a tiny bell came from the box.

Santa is real!

Not Evan A. Mouse

I am one mouse who should need no introduction. I belong among the ranks of the great mice of history, like Dock from Hickory Dickory, and Sir Nipsy, who nibbled the lion free from his net. I, too, changed the course of world events. If it hadn't been for me, there would be no proof that Santa truly exists: no letters to the North Pole, no snacks set out on Christmas Eve.

Oh, you know my story, or at least one version of it. But you don't know my name, and it's all because of Professor Moore's poor penmanship. Let me set the record straight.

I am Evan A. Mouse. Listen to these famous lines and you'll understand my frustration: "'Twas the night before Christmas, when all through the house, not a creature was stirring, not even a mouse." My place in history blurred forever because of missed capital letters and a poorly written vowel. If only the line had been properly penned, "Not Evan A. Mouse," I wouldn't have to defend myself today.

First, my credentials. I am a member of "Mus Legendarius" what the scientific community calls legendary mouse for those of you not up on your Latin. We L.M.'s live extraordinarily long lives and, as I've said before, we find ourselves at key places in history. I was just a youngster in those days, beginning my life's work as a house mouse. It was my job to supervise the Moore household, not an easy task I tell you, because of the four humans who lived there.

First, there was Professor Clement Moore.

My place in history blurred forever.

A teacher, he was forever leaving books, ink wells, and papers all over the house. It took many nibbles in his lecture notes for me to break him of this sloppy habit. Mrs. Moore had the human illness known in our trade as Female Mousaphobia. Her greatest fear was that I would take over her job in the home. When I would quietly remind the Professor to tidy up with a nibble here and there, Mrs. Moore would panic. She would go on a cleaning rampage for a week, just to get me out of the way. Women—who can understand them? The Moores' children, Bartley and Belinda, seemed to be normal enough for their race, loud and noisy. What more can I say? All human children look alike to me.

But back to the night in question, December 24, 1821. If you are familiar with Professor Moore's famous poem, you know how he portrays the events. Let me tell you what really happened. The Professor leads you to believe his home was a calm and peaceful

Professor and Mrs. Moore, Bartley and Belinda.

place that Christmas Eve. Now I ask you, have you ever known any human dwelling to be quiet the day before Christmas? Last minute shopping, wrapping up gifts, gorging on goodies, relatives arriving by the dozens. Anything but peace!

Bartley and Belinda had picked at one another all day. Bartley would pin his little red stocking to the chimney, and Belinda would snatch it down and race around the house, waving it over her head. "Bartley believes in Santy Claus! Ha—ha!" At bedtime, the feathers flew in a horrendous pillow fight as those two jumped from bed to bed. Bartley got in one good swing that knocked out a loose tooth Belinda had been wiggling for weeks.

Professor Moore stomped out of his study, rubbing his temples. Mrs. Moore began shrieking, "I don't care if it is Christmas Eve! If I hear one more peep from the two of you . . ."

Christmas Eve merriment.

I knew there would be no Merry Christmas if I, Evan A. Mouse, didn't do something. I sent the adults to bed with ear plugs and a bottle of aspirin. Getting the younger Moores to settle down took some doing. I used the oldest trick in the House Mouse Book of Human Child Management—bribery. You recall Professor Moore's line, something about sugarplums? I promised massive amounts of candy to the child who could fall asleep first. It worked like a charm.

At last, the household was quiet. I retreated to my observatory up on the roof where I had a first-rate telescope. The clear night promised to provide good viewing. I was looking at the constellation Orion when a strange movement in the heavens caught my eye. Fascinated, I watched as the speck darted from one planet to another. A careful recording of the movements showed that the speck, whatever it was, traveled to Mercury, Venus, and Mars in less than two hours. At

Ready for a long winter's nap.

that point, the speck turned and headed directly for Earth. "Professor Moore should witness this phenomenon!" I thought, and made a mad dash to his bedroom.

The aspirin I had given him earlier had done its job. The Professor was out cold. He claims that a noise outside the house woke him up that night. Might I remind you of the ear plugs he wore to bed? Only I remember that it took a swift bite on the big toe to wake that man up! By the time the two of us poked our heads out the bedroom window, the speck had become large enough to identify. Instantly, I knew I was seeing first-hand something only whispered of in the halls of mousedom. It was the Great One himself, Santus Nikolais, Santa Claus. For generations, we legendary mice had come close to proving his existence, but no one had ever actually seen him in the flesh. And now I, Evan A. Mouse, was standing on the threshold of a major scientific breakthrough.

"Professor Moore should see this!"

The way Professor Moore tells the story, the reindeer were lively and quick that night, and Santa called each one lovingly by name. But my memory has not failed. Fame and Fortune have not clouded my mind. Those reindeer barely made it up to our rooftop. They were totally exhausted. It was the tail end of their North American route. Santa himself practically fell out of the sleigh. "Um-a- Crasher. No, um, I mean, Cruncher . . . No, no, you. .what's your name? Um, reindeer . . . stay here and don't move until I get back!" Santa's scolding wasn't necessary. The minute their hooves had touched our roof, those deer were down and dozing. After three tries, Santa got his sack of toys up on his back and trudged over to our chimney. Somewhere south of New York, he had run into foul weather. His suit was plastered with sticky red mud. Messy, but it did make the trip down the chimney a quick one!

Those reindeer barely made it up to our roof.

Downstairs, Professor Moore and I got our first close look at the Living Legend. The Professor remembers twinkling eyes and a nose red like a cherry. My superior powers of observation led me to notice more details. The Great One was suffering from a nasty cold. His eyes were watering, and he frequently wiped his runny nose on a handkerchief. Once again, I sprang into action, pushing Santa into the Professor's easy chair. First I filled the children's stockings, then I served Santa some hot chicken soup. Those few moments of rest and a dry pair of socks made all the difference that night.

I am convinced that Santa would not have been able to finish his route if I had not been there to give first aid.

Only one task remained, and that was to get the Good Gentleman back up the chimney to his transportation. Santa jumped, the Professor and I pushed from below, but it was hopeless. Finally, I pulled down the trap

A nasty cold!

door to the attic and helped Santa climb out onto the roof. The reindeer galloped into lift-off. Imagine my thrill as we heard these words echo across the night sky:

"Happy Christmas to all at Professor Moore's house,

Special thanks to my good friend, Evan A. Mouse!"

The rest, as they say, is history. The Professor decided to write up his observations and a newspaper printed the article in 1822. Soon, people all over the world believed in Santa Claus and loving and giving. But who gets the credit for all this? Not Evan A. Mouse. All I want is a simple correction:

"Twas the night before Christmas, when all through the house Not a creature was stirring, not Evan A. Mouse!"

All I want is a simple correction!

Today was Christmas Cake Day!

Pepper Cakes

Hear, brethren, hear;
The hour of six is come.
Keep pure each heart,
Bring peace to every home.

Anna Aust woke to the sound of six long blasts on the watchman's conch shell horn. She hated to leave her warm nest of quilts, but then she remembered. Today was Christmas Cake Day!

Anna threw back the heavy covers and swung her feet down. Shivering in her thin linen shift, she reached for the woolen stockings she kept under her pillow in the wintertime. Anna thought there was nothing worse than bare feet on freezing floorboards. With her toes safe in the warm stockings, she ran across the room to where her petticoat and jacket hung from a peg on the wall. She yanked the ankle-length skirt down over her shift and stuck her feet into heavy leather shoes. Next came the fitted blouse called a jacket. Anna moved to the window so she could see to lace up the ribbon that kept the blue jacket closed in front. Around her neck she tied a white scarf called a handkerchief. Running a comb through her long hair, she quickly pinned it up on the back of her neck with hairpins. Last of all, she put on the white linen cap that all the girls and women of Salem wore, and tied the red ribbons under her chin.

The twelve-year old girl flew downstairs and through the kitchen to the back porch where a pitcher of icy water stood on the wash stand. The cold splashes took her

Anna dressed quickly in the cold bedroom.

breath away, and it felt good to sit down at the kitchen table in front of the open fire. Her parents were waiting for her.

"Has my daughter forgotten how to walk, in a manner befitting a proper young Moravian lady?" Brother Gottfried Aust leaned over and kissed Anna on the forehead.

Anna blushed. "I'm sorry, Papa. But today's Christmas Cake Day, and I get to stay home from school to help Mama with the cakes!"

Brother Aust couldn't keep a small smile from dancing at the corners of his mouth. "I like your mother's cakes, too, Anna. But let us not forget the reason why she makes them. It is to share with others the joy of this holy season."

Anna joined hands with her mother and father in prayer before another day of hard work in Salem, a Moravian settlement in the wilderness of North Carolina.

Anna's first task was to stir the giant bowl

"Walk like a young Moravian lady."

of stiff brown dough. As she waited with a wooden spoon, her mother measured out the ingredients: butter, brown sugar, molasses, flour, salt, soda. From drawers in a tiny chest came the precious spices from faraway places that gave Christmas cookies their "bite." Cinnamon, ginger, cloves, a pinch of nutmeg, and just a dash of allspice.

"Is it time for the secret ingredient, Mama?" Anna asked eagerly. Her mother nodded and reached for the pot resting on the hearth. Slowly she poured out a cup of coffee left from breakfast and added it to the bowl of dough. Anna stirred carefully so she wouldn't splash.

Every cook in Salem had a secret recipe for Christmas cakes, some extra touch that she felt made her cakes the best. Mothers passed their secrets on to daughters, but no one outside the family was supposed to know exactly what made the cookies so good. Some cooks made mild Christmas cakes. Others

"Is it time for the secret ingredient?"

added so much ginger, the cookies would sting your tongue. Sister Aust took pride in the fact that her Christmas cakes were a perfect blend of sweetness and spiciness, with the coffee adding a mysterious rich flavor her neighbors all seemed to like. At every Christmas gathering, Mama's cakes always disappeared first!

It was time to knead the dough. Mama took three or four handfuls of flour and dropped them on the tabletop. She would turn the dough out onto the flour and then press, and push, and punch, and squeeze until the dough felt just right. It was always hard work. At that moment, Johann Krause walked in, carrying an arm load of wood.

"Brother Aust told me to bring you some more firewood," the young man said. "He's had me chopping wood for the pottery all morning." The apprentice stacked the split logs in a big box next to the hearth, then turned to see what the women were doing.

It was time to knead the dough.

"Cake Day!" he cried, and bent down over the table. Before Anna knew what was happening, Johann took a deep breath and puffed on the pile of flour. He dashed out of the kitchen, laughing.

Mama and Anna looked at each other. Both of them were covered with white powder, on their faces and on their necks, down their aprons, all over their arms and hands, even on the tops of their shoes.

"The rascal!" Sister Aust chuckled. "It's time we taught that young man a lesson. And I think I know just how to do it!"

Johann Krause worked with Papa in the pottery shed, learning how to shape and fire clay into the jugs, pots, and bowls that the people of Salem used every day. He was a good worker, Papa said, but he still had some growing up to do, even though he was already seventeen.

In the three years that Johann had been with the Austs, he had pulled hundreds of

"The rascal!" sister Aust chuckled.

pranks, especially on Mama. Anna remembered when he tied a broom to Mama's apron strings as she stood working in the kitchen. When she moved, the broom hit her on the back-side! Another time, Johann turned a pig into the house. Mud got all over Mama's nice clean rooms, and Johann had to scrub the walls and floors. Last summer, Mama left three berry pies on the windowsill to cool when Johann came along and ate up all three. But Mama never stayed mad at him for very long. You just had to like someone who enjoyed good food as much as Brother Johann, Mama said.

"Anna, bring me the spice chest."

Sister Aust took a big pinch of black pepper from one of the little drawers and began to knead it into a handful of the cookie dough. When the dough was ready, she used a heavy wooden rolling pin to flatten it out. She rolled and rolled and rolled, until the handful of dough was spread paper thin.

Brother Johann certainly liked to eat!

"Get the Christmas cake cutters and the pans, Anna."

The girl was horrified. "Mama, that was pepper! What are you doing?"

Sister Aust looked up from the rolling pin long enough to grin at her daughter. "You know how much Brother Johann likes Christmas cakes. We are going to make some special ones for him. He won't be able to eat too many of these cakes!" And she sprinkled another pinch of black pepper on the rolled-out dough.

Anna used the old tin cookie cutters that had come from Germany to cut shapes in the spicy dough: hearts, stars, rabbits, pigs, horses, trees.

Carefully, so the thin dough wouldn't tear, her mother lifted the shapes with a knife and placed them on baking sheets. These went into the brick oven at the side of the fireplace, where white-hot coals had been raked flat to bake the cakes evenly. Anna's job was to watch the pans. Christmas cakes

"Mamma, that's pepper!"

were so thin, they would burn if you left them in the oven a minute too long.

But these cakes didn't burn. They turned a nice, rich, spicy brown, and Sister Aust used a long wooden handle to pull the baking sheet from the oven. After the cakes had been out for a minute, she lifted them off with a knife and set them on a plate to cool. They were beautiful-looking Christmas cakes, wafer thin, with crispy edges. Who would ever guess they were loaded with black pepper?

Mother and daughter giggled together, then broke a cookie in half. Anna ate her piece first. She clutched her throat and ran to the water bucket on the back porch. Sister Aust took a tiny nibble and smiled. She would save these pepper cakes for just the right moment, and then wouldn't Brother Johann be surprised!

It took the rest of the day to finish the baking. Anna and her mother rolled and cut and packed up more than a bushel of cook-

They were beautiful Christmas cakes.

ies, enough to share with every guest who might visit during Christmas. Moravian hospitality had made the town of Salem famous, so there were always plenty of visitors.

As Christmas drew near, the bustling town got even busier. People still had everyday chores: milking cows, chopping wood, hauling water, cooking meals. But in between the chores, there was special work to do. The highlight of the holiday in Salem was the Christmas Eve lovefeast. This was a candlelight service held in the Moravian church, with wonderful singing and music. During the lovefeast, everyone, young and old alike, ate a sweetened bun and drank a mug of coffee fixed with milk and sugar. This showed that the people felt like one big family, together in love.

During December, the ladies of Salem filled molds with beeswax to make candles for the service. Others baked the big fluffy buns that would be served. Fathers and sons

Everyone awaited the Christmas lovefeast.

practiced Christmas carols on trumpets, trombones, French horns or flutes. And there were choirs for every age group, so there was special music to learn.

Everyone in the Aust household had a church job this Christmas Eve. Anna was going to sing in the girls' choir, and Sister Aust was a "diener," a lovefeast server. Even Johann Krause would be serious for one night, holding a heavy tray of steaming mugs for the ladies to hand out. But this Christmas, it was Brother Aust, Papa, who had the most important job of all. Every year, a trumpeter was chosen to open the lovefeast service. He would stand on the balcony over the front door of the church and play hymns. This signalled that the service was about to begin. Papa felt very honored.

The day was a busy one. At their afternoon Vesper meal of cake and tea, Mama reminded Anna and Papa that they would not have supper until after the lovefeast.

Papa was to play the first hymn.

She packed her white dinner dress in a basket and went to the church to begin brewing coffee. Anna had to go to one last choir rehearsal, and Papa was going to stay at home and practice his trumpet-playing. They would not meet again until after each one had finished his or her part in the lovefeast.

Two hours later, the people of Salem began gathering outside the door of the church for the Christmas Eve service. Anna stood with the other girls her age and waited for her father to play. It was cold! What was Papa waiting for? She looked up at the balcony. Papa held his trumpet in one hand; with the other, he was covering his mouth and coughing. He coughed and sputtered, and coughed some more. He raised the horn up to his lips, but had to stop and cough again. People standing near Anna began shuffling their feet and whispering. Papa coughed again, but finally got the breath he needed to blow into the trumpet. The first note wavered.

What was wrong with papa?

Was Papa going to be all right? By the third note, he was fine, and the clear bright song rang in the night air.

Anna always loved Christmas Eve. Organ music, the carols, green branches at the windows, the strong smell of coffee, and most of all, candles. During the last song, the dieners handed a candle to each person in the church. Candlelight made even plain faces beautiful on Christmas Eve, Anna thought, as she looked around the room at her Salem friends and neighbors.

The peaceful hush of the lovefeast stayed with her all the way home. She met her parents outside the church and they walked silently down the dark street. But Anna remembered the minute they opened the door to their house.

"Papa, what was wrong with you? Why were you coughing so much? Why couldn't you play the trumpet? Mama, did you hear about Papa? What was it, Papa?"

The dieners handed a candle to each person.

Brother Aust didn't say a word. He marched into the kitchen and picked up a tin bucket of Christmas cakes. He looked at Mama and Anna with fierce eyes.

"Oh, Gottfried," Mama breathed. "You didn't!"

Papa's eyes just grew darker.

"We put black pepper in those cakes to play a trick on Johann," Mama said. "Gottfried, I hid the bucket away so no one would eat them by mistake."

It turned out that Papa had gotten hungry right before time to go to church.

He prowled around the kitchen until he found the cookies Mama and Anna had fixed for Johann. The black pepper tickled and burned his throat badly, so he had a hard time playing the hymns for the Christmas Eve service.

Anna could feel bubbles of laughter bursting inside her throat, but she didn't make a sound. She could tell Papa wasn't ready to

"Oh Gottfried, you didn't!"

laugh about pepper Christmas cakes yet.
Maybe next Christmas, but not now!

Papa ate Brother Johann's pepper cakes!

I used to think Santa was just for kids.

The Fleet

Hey, I used to think Santa Claus was just for little kids, too. That's before I saw The Fleet with my very own eyes. It all started when my dad announced we would be spending Christmas with Uncle George, Aunt Rosa, and the monkeys, uh, I mean, cousins.

"Christmas in the country will be wonderful," my mother said. "We can have a nice old-fashioned holiday. No crowds, no traffic jams, just peace and quiet."

Peace? Quiet? Mom must have had someone else's cousins in mind, because ours yell louder than a squad of cheerleaders. Even when they're not rowdy, they're noisy. It's hard to believe three kids can make so much noise doing normal everyday things. BLAM! Oh, that was only sweet little Jason putting his storybook away. CRASH! Isn't it nice how Christine can stack the dirty dishes? KA-BOOM!! That's Danny, hanging his coat in the closet.

With Christmas just days away, the noise level at Uncle George's house rose a few hundred decibels when we arrived from the city. Those kids were excited about everything: the Christmas tree we brought on the top of our car, the cookies Mom fixed, the mysterious packages Dad unloaded from the trunk. Every little thing about Christmas got those kids more and more excited. Actually, it was kind of fun to watch all the commotion. I'm an only child, so things stay pretty calm around our apartment.

But there was one noise at Uncle George's I never could get used to, and that was the

Christmas got these kids excited.

sound of horses at night. Uncle George and Aunt Rosa have two, J.R. and Pounder. On nights when it doesn't get too cold, the horses stay out in the pasture. Even with the bedroom windows closed, you can hear those horses snorting and snuffling all night long. And if they get to feeling frisky, it's even worse. They gallop around the pasture, and their hooves sound like drumbeats, only louder. So much louder, the bed shakes. The first time I ever slept in Danny's room, I thought those horses were going to break down the window and charge right into the house. Danny hasn't let me forget it, either. He calls me a scaredy cat city slicker.

This visit was no different. We got our pajamas on and climbed into Danny's bunk beds. After lights-out, that kid always talks my ear off until he falls asleep. Mom says it's because he looks up to me, me being the oldest cousin and all. This time, Danny was full of talk about their horses.

I heard horses, all night.

"We'll have to go see J.R. and Pounder first thing in the morning, Adam. Dad and I have really been working with them the last couple of weeks. Boy, just wait until you see 'em run, you're gonna love it. Oh, but I almost forgot! You're a scaredy cat city slicker! You don't like J.R. and Pounder, do you, Adam. Well, we'll cure you of that this Christmas. We'll get some apples and go to the barn right after breakfast, and I'll let you feed J.R. and Pounder yourself. Would you like that, Adam? You think a city slicker can learn to do that? Adam? Are you asleep, Adam?"

I didn't say a word. Finally, Danny rolled over, and in a few minutes I could hear his soft regular breathing. At least I wouldn't have to listen to any more of his blabbermouth. But what he said about the horses worried me. My uncle and his whole family are horse-crazy, and they think everybody else should be, too. J.R. and Pounder are nice, I just don't want to get up too close. I'm

"You should see J.R. and Pounder go!"

perfectly fine sitting on the fence, watching.

Da-Da-DUM! Da-Da-DUM! Da-Da-DUM!
Da-Da-DUM!

The sound of horses galloping outside in the pasture kept me awake long into the night.

At breakfast the next morning, the conversation was all about J.R. and Pounder.

"I want to show you the colts," Uncle George said to my dad. "They're four years old now. High-spirited, but gentle enough for the kids to drive. We've been hitching them to the cart for a while now. It' s a pretty sight to see when they take off down the track."

Uncle George was right. J.R. and Pounder were pretty, with their heads up and their necks arched. Their glossy brown coats shone in the winter sun, and their black manes and tails blew in the wind. Dad and I perched on the fence and watched Danny hitch them to a buggy. He climbed in, and away they went. The horses' heads stretched

J.R. and Pounder sped around the track.

out, and their slender legs flashed as they sped around the track.

"What are you going to do with them now that they're trained, George?" my dad asked. "I'm sure a matched pair like this would sell for big bucks."

Uncle George looked startled. "Sell J.R. and Pounder? Why, that would be like selling Danny, Christine, and Jason! Besides, they've been reserved for The Fleet this year. Okay, Danny, bring 'em in!" and Uncle George jogged off to help with the harnesses.

I looked over at Dad. "The Fleet? I thought a fleet was a bunch of ships. Is Uncle George sending J.R. and Pounder to the Navy?"

"Beats me," Dad shrugged.

The days before Christmas went by in a blur of cooking, eating, singing, watching sappy old movies on TV, tramping through the woods to cut holly and pine, doing chores with the cousins. Not at all the kind of Christmas you have in the city, but fun any-

Tramping through the woods

way. Once, I remembered to ask Danny about the horses and The Fleet.

"You'll find out soon enough," he grinned.

I attacked him with kernels of popcorn we were stringing for the Christmas tree. "Tell me what The Fleet is, you country bumpkin, you!"

He counter-attacked with one of Aunt Rosa's throw pillows. "No way, stuck-up scaredy cat city slicker!"

Christine and Jason looked in to see what was going on. In seconds, the battle turned into a war. It was great. Kids rolling all over the floor, everyone tickling everyone else, screaming, shrieking, giggling. But then somebody knocked over a lamp and it fell with a crash. The grown-ups rushed in.

"You kids cut that out right now! Danny, Adam, I'm surprised at you two,"

Uncle George said. "You're old enough to know better. Another free-for-all like this and you'll have to miss the Star Walk."

The battle turned into a war.

"Dad, you wouldn't!" Danny howled. "Especially not this year! We've got to see The Fleet!"

I still didn't know what The Fleet was, but I knew all about the Star Walk.

It's a Munson family Christmas tradition. Dad and Uncle George did it when they were growing up, and we do it now with our family. Every Christmas Eve, we take a walk outside and look at the stars. Of course, in the city, we have to pick a safe place to walk, and sometimes we don't actually see many stars. But it's a nice time to be by ourselves, to walk and talk. I was looking forward to a Star Walk in the country because I figured it would be a lot different.

The threat of missing the Star Walk kept all of us kids good all the way through Christmas Eve. At last, supper was over. Uncle George got up from the table and grabbed his coat. He motioned for Dad, Danny, and me to come with him. We walked

The Star Walk was a family tradition.

to the barn. Uncle George handed us brushes, currycombs, and cloths.

"We don't have much time to get J.R. and Pounder groomed. Adam, you help me work on Pounder. Danny, show your uncle what to do with J.R."

Groomed for what, I wondered, but Uncle George spoke before I could get the question out.

"Now, Adam, I know you're a little nervous being this close to Pounder. Just come into the stall and let him get used to you."

Before I knew it, I was right in front of Pounder's gigantic face. His huge liquid eyes rolled when he saw me, and his lips moved constantly, showing square yellowish teeth. Pounder's head moved over to my shoulder. He made a little snorting sound and blew on me. I was paralyzed.

Uncle George slapped me on the back. "See there, Pounder likes you. Here, you brush the shoulder and the flank while I work on

I was paralyzed.

his hooves. Use nice long strokes in the same direction that the hair grows."

I couldn't believe it, but Pounder stood there and let us work on him for almost an hour. He was beautiful when we were through, his coat shining, the tangles in his mane and tail all combed out. Uncle George put some oil on a little brush and polished the hooves until they looked like black patent leather. Over in the next stall, Dad and Danny were finished with J.R.

"Now for the final touch," Uncle George said.

He went in the tack room where all the saddles and reins are stored. We heard the jingle of bells. Uncle George brought out two red leather bridles trimmed with ribbons and little silver bells.

"Wow!" Danny exclaimed. "I've never seen those before. Where'd you get 'em, Dad?"

"Special delivery from someplace up North," Uncle George winked.

Pounder let us groom him for almost an hour.

We led J.R. and Pounder into the paddock next to the barn. As Uncle George closed the gate, he reached over with an apple for each horse.

"Tonight's the night, fellas. Do old George proud out there!"

Mom, Aunt Rosa, Christine, and Jason met us by the barn with flashlights and quilts. We went a little ways down a dirt road and climbed up a small hill. The stars were out, and dark farmland stretched all around us. Aunt Rosa passed out the quilts and we sat down in a cozy huddle.

"I see the Big Dipper!" Dad called out.

"Too easy!" said Uncle George. "Bet you can't find Cassiopeia!"

Everybody started pointing out their favorite stars. I learned some new ones I don't think I'd ever seen in the city. From under the quilts, Aunt Rosa produced a thermos of hot chocolate, and we sipped and talked. Finally, Uncle George checked his watch.

"Bet you can't find Cassiopeia!"

"Okay, everybody, it's almost time. Find the Milky Way."

Almost directly overhead, the Milky Way stretched across the sky like a silver highway. Individual stars twinkled in the broad band of light, giving it a magical, sparkling look. Then, from the pasture by the barn, we heard excited snorts and whinnying. We could hear J.R. and Pounder paw at the ground.

"Is something wrong with the horses, George?" Mom asked.

Uncle George didn't answer, he just kept looking back and forth from the pasture up to the Milky Way. Suddenly, his arm shot up.

"Look, there it is! It's The Fleet! They're coming for J.R. and Pounder!"

High up in the sky, galloping across the Milky Way, were hundreds of horses.

Starlight flowed around smooth bodies, and manes blew back in the nightl wind of their speed. Dainty feet seemed to barely touch down as the horses galloped across the sky.

In the sky were hundreds of horses.

We could see all kinds of horses in the herd, sleek Arabians, Clydesdales, quarter horses, thoroughbred racers, even Indian ponies. Each horse wore a red leather bridle like the ones we had put on J.R. and Pounder.

The nickering over in the pasture grew louder. We heard an explosion of hooves hitting the ground. Seconds later, our horses were headed up, galloping through the starry night towards the Milky Way! The herd above us paused and waited for J.R. and Pounder to join them. Then they were off, thundering down the heavenly trail, leaving a cloud of stardust behind. In just a few seconds, they were out of sight. The night sky was peaceful and silent once more, as if nothing had disturbed it for ages.

It took me more than an hour to make sense of all I had seen. Everyone started talking at once, and I asked a million questions. Here, finally, is what I figured out:

1. Most of us have it wrong: Santa uses

It's a great honor to join the Fleet.

horses, not reindeer, for his sleigh.

2. Just on Christmas Eve, the horses chosen for The Fleet can gallop through the air.

3. Santa's journey around the world is so long and difficult, he goes through many teams of fresh horses.

4. Someone from the North Pole had called Uncle George before Christmas and reserved J.R. and Pounder.

5. It is a great honor to be chosen for The Fleet.

6. Once a horse has ridden with The Fleet, he is forever changed.

I might add that once a person has seen The Fleet, he also is forever changed. My opinion of horses has completely changed. They're my favorite animal now. I'm on friendly terms with all the police horses that patrol the city here. I also take Santa Claus very seriously. Believe me, I BELIEVE. After all, I saw the great round-up in the sky with my very own eyes. I don't care how old I get

Horse are my favorite animal now.

to be, every Christmas Eve from now on, you'll find me outside, looking up at the stars.

Wild horses couldn't keep me away!

Every Christmas Eve I look up at the stars.

An empty packing crate for a desk.

Crayon Box Christmas

Late one night, a young girl named Cathy sat up alone, coloring a large wreath she had cut out of cardboard. Boxes and bundles stood piled in the center of the small, dark apartment. Cathy used an empty packing crate for a desk. It was the end of moving day, and it was Christmas Eve.

She girl had lost count of the times she and her mother and her younger sister had moved. Too many, that's for sure. No matter where they moved, nothing changed. Their bad luck just moved with them. This time, the factory where her mother had been working went out of business, so they packed up and drove to a new city. To check out the possibilities, her mother had said. But moving took most of her mother's last paycheck. That meant no money for a Christmas tree or presents, not even a wreath for the front door. That's why Cathy sat up late this evening, coloring the cardboard wreath she had cut from an empty box.

The only light in the room came from a desk lamp she had unpacked. It cast a round golden glow on the surface of the moving crate. In the circle of light gleamed one hundred and thirty-two new crayons, their waxy points sharp and shiny. Crayons were the only good thing about this day, she thought.

The crayons had been a going-away Christmas present from a friend. Because Cathy moved so often, she didn't like to make friends, but this last time she had met someone different. Someone who liked to draw as much as she did, someone who saw

Possibilities in a box of crayons.

possibilities in her pictures. Someone she missed already. Someone who knew she would like a deluxe box of crayons for a present. Cathy had always liked crayons, even after other kids her age had graduated to fancy felt-tip markers and paints. She liked how the crayons looked, lined up in the box like little soldiers standing at attention. She liked their waxy smell, and she liked the names of the colors: goldenrod, carnation pink, sea green, mulberry, raw umber. Most of all, she liked the way crayons felt: the soft paper wrapper, the weight of the round stick in her fingers, the picture ideas that seemed to flow down her arm and into her hand. There were so many possibilities in a new box of crayons.

She worked hard on her coloring. The plan was to finish the cardboard wreath, and then make a large cardboard Christmas tree. If they couldn't afford a real tree, they might as well have a homemade one, cut from the

She finished her home-made decorations.

biggest moving box she could find. At least there would be something special for her sister to see on Christmas morning.

The hours passed, and Cathy colored on. At the stroke of midnight, she had just finished the last ornament on the cardboard Christmas tree when a voice called softly from the open crayon box.

" Psst, girl! Take me out, big girl! I need to talk with you!"

Cathy looked closely at her crayon box. All the crayons looked normal, except for a brown one in the corner, a color she had not used yet. Somehow, that crayon looked glossier than the others, more alive. Carefully, she pulled it up from its spot in the box. The wax stick came to life in her hand, little brown arms and legs sprouting out of the paper wrapper. A sassy brown face grinned at her from under a pointed brown hat.

"Who are you?" Cathy gasped.

"I'm Sepia!"

"I'm Sepia," the little crayon lady chuckled. "See, it says so right on my wrapper."

"You— you're —real!" Cathy couldn't believe she was talking to a crayon.

"Of course I am. How do you think you big people draw pictures?

All by yourselves? With those clumsy giant hands of yours? Don't be ridiculous! We crayon people guide your fingers and make it possible. Why, if it weren't for us, you could not have drawn such a beautiful wreath and Christmas tree tonight."

Cathy thought about this strange idea for a minute. "Well, I thank you then, Miss Sepia," she said slowly. "I'm glad you helped me with the cardboard tree. It's the only one my family is going to have this Christmas."

"Ah, that's where you're wrong," smiled Sepia gently. "On this Night of All Possibilities, my dear child, you have been granted a special favor. Watch!"

Standing in Cathy's palm, Sepia turned

"We crayon people guide your fingers."

and bowed low in the direction of the home-made Christmas tree. Suddenly, streaking from every corner of the dark room, flashes of color gathered above the cardboard cut-out. For a brief second, she could see a shim-mering rainbow, and then the colors melted and sank into her tree. But it was no longer just a crayon tree, it was the largest, green-est, freshest, real Christmas tree Cathy had ever seen!

Next, the brown crayon lady pointed her hat at the girl's cardboard wreath. More fly-ing colors gathered and transformed the art-work into a lovely full circle of real, fragrant evergreens.

The girl stared, first at the real tree and wreath, then at Sepia. "Oh, thank you! Thank you so much!"

Sepia chuckled, "There's more, if you can draw it, my dear. Is it Possible you could do a picture to give to your sister on Christmas morning?"

"Tonight is the night for All Possibilities."

Cathy's eyes opened wide. "You mean . . .?"
Sepia nodded. "Tonight, all the Possibilities in the crayon box will come alive for you. Now, what will you draw for your sister?"

Cathy looked over the crayons waiting in the box. A wonderful Christmas picture started to take shape in her mind. Midnight blue for a dark winter sky, and silver for millions of tiny winking stars. Pearl white for a glistening mountain of snow. Cinnamon brown for the bark of trees loaded with lemon drops and tangerine candies. Ruby red, emerald green, and amethyst for jeweled birds singing in the branches. She reached for her crayons. The picture flowed out of her fingers and onto a piece of the moving box cardboard.

"Excellent," Sepia whispered. She bowed in the direction of the drawing and the winter scene came to life before them. It was so real that Cathy felt snowflakes brush against her cheek, and she heard a ruby car-

She drew a wonderful picture for her sister.

dinal call from a lemon drop tree.

Next, her mother's picture. Cathy closed her eyes for a minute. Then she reached for every warm, comfortable, delicious color in the crayon box. Peach, melon, apricot, violet. Salmon, banana, orchid, clover, and spring green. Beneath her fingers bloomed a bountiful feast in the grass. A nod from Sepia, and piles of luscious fruit filled the room. Carnations and violets and the smell of fresh-baked bread perfumed the air.

The two drawings would make Christmas gifts never to be forgotten.

Now Sepia spoke quickly, "Listen, my dear, before our moment passes. My special gift to you is Seeing Possibilities. You have always been able to See Possibilities in a box of crayons. Now, think larger! Draw a picture of a big, wonderful life for yourself, and live it! Look for all the great possibili. . ."

And the lively little woman turned back into an ordinary brown crayon.

And now a picture for her mother.

Laughter, hugs, and tears of joy greeted Cathy on Christmas morning. Her mother and her younger sister were astonished to see the magnificent real tree and the handsome green wreath on the front door. Even more wondrous were the two special gifts, drawings so real you could taste and touch and smell them. It was an incredible day.

As Cathy lay in bed that night, thoughts of her own Christmas present ran through her head. She touched the crayon under her pillow. Possibilities? And as she fell asleep, a little brown voice seemed to speak in her dreams. "See the Possibilities, my dear! Possibilities for great drawings. Possibilities for new friends. Possibilities for a happy family. Possibilities for you!"

They were amazed to see a real Christmas tree.

December 25, 2102

The Best Christmas Gift
in the Universe

"How does it look, Wringle?" Santa bent over the little man scooping snow into a tester of three clear plastic tubes.

"Too early to tell yet, sir. We should know something in exactly—" Wringle clicked his watch—"47 seconds."

Santa bit nervously on the ends of the bristly white hairs that poked out over his upper lip. "I just have a feeling this is going to be the year."

Wringle peered into the tester. The snow in the first tube was slowly turning a brilliant turquoise blue. The snow in the second tube was orange, and the third tube remained white.

The bulky man and his child-sized assistant stood on top of an industrial complex in New Dawn City, on what had once been the most polluted spot on Planet Earth. The sun was just beginning to peep over the horizon. It was Christmas Day, December twenty-fifth; the year was 2102.

Wringle's watch beeped, and he switched on a thermometer-like probe he had been holding. Inserting it in the tube of turquoise snow, Wringle muttered under his breath, "Come on, baby, give me a Go. Give me a Go for Santa."

Suddenly the probe let out a high-pitched tone and a green light flashed at the top. Wringle's hand shook as he removed the probe.

"You've done it, sir! You've done it!"

"Not so fast, Wringle. We have to pass all three purity tests. What do the other two read?"

"I have a feeling this is the year!"

Wringle repeated the test twice and got the tone and the green flashing light each time. He and Santa stood wordless for a long minute, each gripping the other's hand. Tears filled their eyes. Both men had worked hard and waited long for this moment.

Santa broke the stillness. "Well, we know what we have to do now, Wringle. Let's get to it. I hope you will accompany me to the Christmas Gathering?"

"Oh, sir! I never dreamed . . . What an honor . . . Sir, of course I will come!"

The two grinned at each other and turned to the steaming pink sleigh shuttle parked behind them. Wringle ran to the control panel and clicked on the autocleanser while Santa opened a storage bin at the back of the sleigh. He pulled out eight silver cartridges about the size of bullets.

"Do you think eight atomic reindeer will get us there?" he asked Wringle.

Wringle peered up at the sun. "Yes, sir,

Getting ready for a trip to the sun.

that should push us up at about EV28, plenty of time to make the Gathering."

The sleigh cleansed of snow and mud, stood quivering and hissing ready for its next precious cargo—100% pure Earth snow. Santa and Wringle pulled shovels from the sleigh's tool bin and began loading the white frozen crystals into a huge bag in the hold.

"Bet the guys up at the Pole never thought we would be doing this today," laughed Wringle as he stopped to catch his breath for a second.

"Hm, I hope they are resting by now." Santa said, mopping his forehead. "All the elves worked extra hard this season, including you, Wringle. I've never seen the sleigh packed higher than last night. I'm tired, too. The delivery route seems to get longer each year. But shoveling snow this morning is one job I'm glad to do."

"What do you think the Overlord will say, sir? Will he be surprized? And what about

"This is the one job I'm glad to do!"

the other Santas? What do you think they'll say?"

Santa let out his famous laugh, "Ho, ho, ho! There's only one way to find out, my friend. Let's get cracking!" He dug down deep in the snow.

Half an hour later the sleigh shuttle was filled to the brim with snow and the hatch closed tightly. Inside, Santa and his first mate donned helmets and strapped themselves in for their journey. Exhaustion pressed down on them like a heavy blanket.

"At least we can catch forty winks on the way up," yawned Santa. "This is one Gathering I plan to enjoy."

In a silent sh-oo-sh, the sleigh shuttle lifted from the Earth with seven million pounds of thrust. In a matter of seconds, the ship had achieved Escape Velocity, the speed needed to leave Earth's gravity and to travel to the Sun. Although the human race had made enormous strides in space travel, colo-

Taking a long winter's nap.

nizing the Moon, landing on Mercury and Mars, this journey to the Sun was beyond their realm of belief.

In this advanced civilization, parents still told their children stories about Santa Claus, but they were quaint tales of an old-fashioned rocket that buzzed around the planet delivering packages. What humans didn't know, had never known, was that their Santa was real. His task on their planet went far beyond simply bringing Christmas joy. Their Santa had been sent from the Sun by the Overlord himself to manage, guide, and protect this third member of the solar system. Indeed, the Earthlings knew nothing of the Overlord. They still clung to the idea that theirs was the only life form in the galaxy. In spite of the fact that transmissions arrived daily from other planets. In spite of the fact that their astronauts had stepped over crater cities on Mercury and photographed ice cap colonies on Mars. In

There is life everywhere out there!

spite of the fact that the stories about Santa Claus himself lived on, from the earliest days of recorded Earth history to the present. With all these clues before them, the Earthlings simply could not see, did not want to see, the wealth of life teeming in their solar system.

Now, from this tiny corner of the galaxy, Santa Claus and Wringle made their way toward the Sun. The journey was beyond speed; it was all about light and color. Their ship quickly left the blackness of Earth's atmosphere and entered an interplanetary realm of shifting greens and blues. As the shuttle drew closer and closer to the Sun, the colors blazed brighter and burned away at the tiny vehicle and its riders. Humans had always feared these burning rays. They had tried to keep them out with protective shields, not realizing they were shutting off the very power source that could take them to new worlds and beyond. First, the ship

The sun burned away all that was old.

blazed purple and then red as the temperatures climbed higher and higher. Heading straight for the Sun's corona, the metal hull turned blue-white, burning at degrees inconceivable to Earth's scientists.

Changes were also happening inside the ship. As Santa and Wringle slept on, the heat from outside crept in and burned away at their skin, first turning it brown, then blue-black, and finally, a rainbow color like that of soap bubbles, a shade that mirrored all the colors dancing outside the ship. The intense rays were like a cleansing, a burning away of all that was old and soiled and imperfect. Like butterflies emerging from their cocoons, Santa and Wringle became new creations.

Millions and millions of miles slipped by. Soon, the sleigh's atomic thrust slowed. For a short while, the shuttle rocked in limbo, still moving forward, but slowly and gently. Had Santa and Wringle been awake and

Special delivery to the Imperial Kitchens!

looking out a porthole, they would have seen eleven other ships also rocking, like gentle giant cradles. Fingers of solar wind reached out and tickled the ships, drawing them gently ever closer to the surface of the Sun. Each ship hovered above the corona until, with a whoosh, the dark hollow of a sunspot would open and the ship would dive deep in to the Sun's core. Whoosh, whoosh, whoosh, twelve times a different sunspot opened and twelve times a ship vanished from the corona, leaving a brilliant tail of energy blazing behind.

Deep in the core, the shuttles docked and the hatches opened. Down from the ships came the twelve Santas of the solar system, rested and with faces rainbow bright. There was Santa Claus from Earth and Santa Maus from Mercury; Taus and Draus from Venus and Mars. From Jupiter came Faus; Paus from Saturn; Kaus, Jaus, and Baus from Uranus, Neptune, and Pluto. Santas

The twelve Santas of the solar system.

from planets not yet known to Earth were also there: Gaus, Naus, and Vaus from Tarsus, Omom, and Ghee. Their rainbow faces sparkled as they greeted one another with hugs and handshakes. There had been many long lonely days since the last Christmas Gathering.

Behind them an army of elves swarmed over the sleighs, unloading the precious cargo brought by each Santa. There were jewel eggs from the rings

of Saturn, volcanic honey from Mars, meteor beetles from Omom, and more. All the delights of the solar system were now shooting down a transport tube to the Overlord's Imperial Kitchens. After the serious work of the Gathering was done, what a Christmas feast these Santas would have!

Claus and Wringle watched as elves pushed their huge thermal bag of snow out onto the transport tube beltway. The clasp on the top of the bag remained sealed.

All the delights of the solar system.

Wringle giggled, "Tee-hee! No one knows, do they? I'll bet they think you've brought reindeer moss again! Hee-hee!! They sure will be surprized at the Christmas banquet! They don't know how hard you've worked, cleaning up Earth's pollution so the sn—"

Claus clapped a hand over Wringle's mouth and turned to a Santa walking over to their sleigh. "Greetings, Brother Gaus. How goes it on Tarsus?"

The two Santas walked away together, discussing the work on their planets. Wringle restrained himself until they were out of sight and then took off down the beltway after the bag of snow. With a flying leap, he landed right on top of the bag and rode grandly down to the Kitchens. After all, he giggled to himself, he was delivering the Christmas present of the evening!

Solemn tones echoing from a gamma ray organ brought silence to the Imperial Solarium. Reverently, the Santas bowed their

Santa and Wringle became new creations.

heads as the Overlord entered and took his place at the head of the polished meteorite table.

"Praise be to our High Lord Creator," said the Overlord.

"The Father and Mother of all Life, our High Lord Creator," answered the twelve Santas.

Folding his old sun gold hands across his chest, the Overlord gave each Santa a long probing look. This ancient being who ruled the solar system for the High Lord Creator had been a Santa himself long long ago. He knew the tears and the thorns each Santa faced in guiding his planet. It was not an easy job.

One by one, the Santas presented their reports. The Overlord listened to accounts of war among the insect-men of Mars, and that a mystery disease was killing the diamond trees of Pluto. He heard how Santa Vaus had taught the Gheeites to sing, and that Jaus and his Neptuners were finally at peace.

One by one the Santas presented their reports.

Then it was time for Earth's account. The Overlord turned to Santa Claus, "How are things on our dear third planet, Claus?"

Santa Claus told of medical cures for that dreaded Earthling disease, the bad cold. He talked of schools where all of Earth's children learned rudiodeology. He told how the lost forests of Sherwood had been replanted, and that the Earthlings at last were recycling their atomic waste. Santa Claus stopped speaking and looked down.

"Is that all, Claus?" the Overlord asked, searching the Santa's face with his wise old eyes.

It was all Santa Claus could do to keep the secret of the pure Earth snow from showing on his face.

"Hm, I see. Well, Claus, the High Lord Creator will be pleased with little Earth. Good work."

The meeting continued until all reports had been given. At last, the Overlord stood.

"Is that all, Claus?"

"Well done, my loyal workers. Let us proceed to the Imperial Banquet Hall."

The wonderful sights and heavenly smells that awaited them in the Hall were beyond words. Tables piled high with treats from every planet lined the room. Stomachs began to rumble as the Santas eyed the delicious dishes.

But before the feasting came the presentation of the Christmas Gift to the Overlord.

Whispers buzzed around the room.

"What is the Gift to be?"

"Which planet sent it this time?"

"I haven't heard a word about the Gift!"

"We do have a Gift for the Overlord, don't we?"

"Where is the Gift?"

Wringle stepped proudly out of the crowd, carrying a covered serving dish. This was his moment of glory. With a flourish, he bowed low before the

Overlord and then lifted the lid. There,

Wringle's moment of glory!

piled high on the dish, was a treat not seen at the Christmas Gathering for over a century—sparkling white snow cream from Earth, a frozen concoction of cream and sugar and pure snow. The most delectable dish Planet Earth had to offer.

The buzzing began again, this time louder and with great excitement.

"He's finally done it"

"Congratulations, Claus! Good work!"

"Imagine, after all these years, clean snow!"

Silently, the Overlord reached for the spoon held out by Wringle. He lifted a scoop up to his lips and slowly tasted the snow cream with eyes closed. No one dared breathe. At long last, he opened his eyes and smiled.

"The best Christmas Gift in the Universe!" he proclaimed and held the dish high amid cheers from all the elves and Santas.

Over the heads of the crowd, the Overlord and Santa Claus looked into each other's

"The best Christmas gift in the Universe!"

eyes. Each knew what an accomplishment this was. At long last, Earth was free from the curse of pollution. Santa and the Earthlings had given a healthy planet back to the Universe.

The High Lord Creator be praised!

Earth was free from the curse of pollution.

The longest, darkest night of the year.

John Franklin's Story

It was December twenty-first, the longest, darkest, stillest night of the year at the North Pole. Months had passed since the animals had seen true sunlight. Up until a few weeks ago, a lighter shade of gray would lift the blackness for a few minutes at noon. But now, not a particle of light penetrated the cold. The dark sky bent down to the ice below in a frozen dome of silence.

It was to escape this silence that the animals gathered now outside a small solitary house. Built from blocks cut out of packed snow and hardened by wind and frost, the house had a single large room with a window on one side and a smoke hole in the roof. Attached were several smaller rooms used for storage. A long, low tunnel served as a passageway into the house, and from out of this tunnel crawled a man.

Wearing heavy fur garments, the man walked over to the animals waiting at a tall wall of ice.

"Ah, it is good to see you, little friends. Thank you for joining me tonight.

The strength of your friendship will cheer me on the long journey I am about to make. Knowing you are here waiting, I will return home with a gladdened heart."

The animals watched the man with loving eyes, but they kept their distance in quiet respect. The man continued speaking, looking out into the dark sky as if he had forgotten the animals were there. He paced back and forth in front of the wall of ice. It was taller than the man himself, and it glistened

"Your love will cheer me on my journey!"

with light reflected from a small fire burning at its base. Colors from the flames danced across the frozen screen. As the man talked, pictures seemed to take shape up on the wall, images that sprang from the man's mind, fed by the firelight.

The animals were spell-bound by the colors and patterns that flowed across the screen. Motionless, they listened as the man told the story they had heard every Christmas for more than one hundred years.

"As you know, friends, my name is not really Santa Claus. It is John Franklin, and I was born in England in 1786. I first came to the Arctic region as a young midshipman, serving under Captain Matthew Flinders. We were exploring the waters of the Northern Territory, and the frozen beauty of this part of the world seeped into my bones. I determined to make polar exploration my life's work. I knew I could find a shipping route through the Arctic that would connect

"I came to the Arctic as a young sailor."

East and West. I knew somewhere up here, a sailing ship from England could thread its way through the icebergs and come out on the other side of the world."

The man paused for breath. The animals watched, fascinated by pictures of a fifteen-year old boy joining the British Navy, climbing the ropes on a large sailing ship, watching ice floes pass by. The man continued his story.

"It took twenty-five years, but I succeeded. On my third expedition to the Arctic, with a crew of 130 men, I sailed around Greenland and found a path through the islands north of Canada. The path led to the Eastern Hemisphere, but I did not gain fame and fortune for this discovery. Ice crushed my ship, and my men were lost in the freezing waters. Somehow, I alone survived. I was flung unconscious onto a large drifting floe and found a day later by an Eskimo hunting party. Only a thread of life remained in my

The Eskimos brought me to their camp.

frozen body. The Eskimos wrapped me in skins and paddled back to their camp. It is only because of their kindness that I am alive today."

The screen now danced with images familiar to the small creatures of the Pole: scenes of kayaks and dog sleds, Eskimo families building snow houses, hunting parties looking for seals, walruses, and polar bears. The animals watched as the wall showed how the man once known as John Franklin slowly learned the art of survival in the frozen North. They saw him bid farewell to his Eskimo friends and head out on his own. Driving a team of eight dogs, he traveled across the ice day after frozen day.

"Something was drawing me North," John Franklin said. "I had hopes of making my way back to civilization, and hitching a ride home to England and my wife. But the ice was bad, and I could not make the dogs run in any direction but north. And it felt good,

"Something inside me kept pushing me north."

somehow right, to be going north, north, always north. After endless days of travel, the urge I felt inside pushing me on, suddenly stopped. It was as clear as a voice in my head, telling me to stop now, this was the place."

With his hands, the man indicated to the animals that they were sitting at the very spot where his journey ended. They watched reflections of John Franklin building a house, caring for his team of sled dogs, hunting the large beasts of the North for food and skins, sitting alone through the long dark polar winter.

"It was during that first year that I learned to carve ice crystals. My hunting had gone well, so I had enough food and clothing to last the winter. It was my mind I was worried about: no books to read, no human to talk to. In desperation, I picked up a knife and began carving. The face of my dear wife Elizabeth took shape in my hands.

"Everything I loved, I carved in the ice."

Cut from the clearest iceberg crystal, the carving shimmered with inner light. In my loneliness, it seemed as if the crystal figure brought Elizabeth nearer to me, as if somehow our thoughts met across the frozen miles."

"That's how I started my crystal collection. Every day, I cut something new out of the ice, something I missed from my life back home. Faces of friends, good food, my pet collie dog, books, tools I could have put to great use in the snow, even toys I remembered from my childhood. All the things I loved became ice carvings. Soon my snow house was crowded with crystals, and I had to build a storeroom on the side."

"Finally, this night, December 21, the longest night of the winter came. I knew in a few weeks the sun would slowly return. The brief Arctic summer would be the only time I could travel south. If I waited too late to begin the journey home, I would be

"It was the only time I could travel south."

trapped by the ice again. My chances of making it were slim, but the voice in my head spoke again, urging me to go now. I loaded a sled with food and skins; at the last minute I threw in a bundle of carvings. My dogs were eager to run after their long rest, and the sled flew like the wind."

"Mile after mile zipped by. Neither I nor the dogs seemed to tire. We ran all that first night and well into the next day. It was when I first pulled on the lines to stop the dogs that I realized we had actually been flying through the air. Just the wind behind us, I thought, but each day was the same. We flew high into the sky and we covered incredible distances. Already, after only three days of travel, I could see the lights of civilization below us. "

"I noticed that the atmosphere had grown uncomfortably warm. The odor of wet marsh filled me with sudden distaste. I had no desire to stop at the suffocating lands slip-

"At first I thought it was just the wind."

ping by beneath us. I missed the keen crisp air of the North. But what about Elizabeth, and England? I pointed the dogs east, and in a little while, the hills of Scotland came into view. Just a few moments more, and I was over London. Everyone and everything that I loved lay below."

Here John Franklin stopped speaking, emotion choking off his words. The animals waited.

The pictures on the wall shifted now and they showed a woman, weeping. It was Elizabeth, John's wife. She prayed and wrote letters. She went to see important people, people who could send ships to look for her husband.

Three times men went north searching for John Franklin; three times they came back, defeated by the ice. At last, Elizabeth stopped crying. But always, she sat alone, reliving memories of her husband.

"Elizabeth, dear Elizabeth. I couldn't come home. As much as I wanted to be with you, I

"Elizabeth sent out ships to look for me."

felt an even stronger call, a call to return north. I knew then I belonged forever at the Pole, but I wanted to reach out, dear heart, to let you feel my love once more. I did the only thing I could think to do. Grabbing the bundle of ice crystals, I flung them over the sleeping city. Somehow, I hoped, at least one crystal would find its way to you, Elizabeth."

Colors shimmered on the wall of ice behind the man. In shadowy images, the animals could see John's ice carvings drifting down on the houses of London. The few people who were awake rushed out to see the shimmering gifts that were falling from the clouds. Some folk looked up, and they caught just a glimpse of John's sled and his team of huskies as they vanished in the northern sky. The city buzzed that Christmas with talk about St. Nick. People swore they had actually seen a sleigh and eight tiny reindeer; they claimed it was Santa Claus in the flesh. At one house, John's present worked

Shimmering gifts fell from the clouds.

the magic he hoped for: Elizabeth went to sleep with a tiny glass figurine clutched in her hand, her heart somehow eased by its crystalline beauty.

"That was almost a hundred and fifty years ago," John told his animal friends. "I have made the same trip every year since then. Breathing the pure Arctic air keeps me young. People all over the world know me as Santa Claus, and I scatter my ice carvings as I fly. Something happens to the crystals when they fall through the air, for by the time they land, they have become actual presents. When the journey is over, I return here to the North Pole, to watch the world on my screen and to carve from ice the gifts most needed by people below. Some gifts become playthings, to bring happiness to little children. Other gifts are much harder to carve, the gifts of food and health and peace for a suffering world."

"It is a difficult job, but I am content. I know

"I am neither the first nor the last Santa."

it is my time to be Santa Claus. I am not the first, nor will I be the last. I am simply one link in a very long chain. Patiently studying my wall one year, I was shown the Santas of ages past. The screen revealed that at the very moment I got lost in the Arctic, the Santa before me went to his eternal reward. I know that one day, the next Santa will appear, and I will go to be at last with my Elizabeth."

"As each new exploration team approaches the Pole, I ask, 'Is it time? Are you the one?' Robert Peary, Matthew Henson, Richard Byrd, Vivian Fuchs—many travelers have come and gone; still I wait. "

The man the world knew as Santa Claus slumped in silence before the wall of ice. His task seemed overwhelming: to bring the most needed gifts to a world very much in need, year after year after year. The animals rushed to surround their friend. With nips and licks and snuffles, they soon had him standing straight again.

240